Fostering Champ

by

Sandi Petee

Bloomington, IN Milton Keynes, UK

AuthorHouse™
1663 Liberty Drive, Suite 200
Bloomington, IN 47403
www.authorhouse.com
Phone: 1-800-839-8640

AuthorHouse™ UK Ltd.
500 Avebury Boulevard
Central Milton Keynes, MK9 2BE
www.authorhouse.co.uk
Phone: 08001974150

© 2007 Sandi Petee. All rights reserved.

No part of this book may be reproduced, stored in a retrieval system, or transmitted by any means without the written permission of the author.

First published by AuthorHouse 8/21/2007

ISBN: 978-1-4343-1175-7 (sc)

Library of Congress Control Number: 2007903056

Printed in the United States of America
Bloomington, Indiana

This book is printed on acid-free paper.

Dedications

For my amazing children, Kylie and Tyler- My love for you is unending. I am so proud to be your mother. May you always follow your dreams and passions!

For my Mother, Nancy- Thank you for being my cheerleader, my teacher, my counselor, my role model and my friend. I love you!

For my Husband, Brad- Without you, this would have only remained a dream. Thank you for putting up with me as I pursue my passions! I love you.

For Jamie and Jim- Thank you for the many years of loyal friendship, your encouragement and your wisdom in helping make this dream a reality. The animals and I love you both!

Finally, this book is dedicated to all the stray and shelter animals who are hoping for someone to love, care for and watch over them until they find a forever home!

Chapter 1

A Girl's Best Friend

Madison Sarnicki was feeling like the weather today- sad and gloomy. She sat looking out the back car window, watching the raindrops merge into tiny rivers flowing down the glass. She was on her way to her grandmother's funeral. The loss of her Grandmother made her sad, but even worse was leaving her beloved dog behind.

If it had been any other visit, the family dog, *her* dog, would have come with them. Because her grandmother had died, her mom and dad felt it would be best if he stayed behind this time. Madison was crushed! She had never, ever been separated from Bogey for more than a day, and now she would be away from him four days! It just didn't seem fair.

What was she going to do for four whole days while her parents took care of the funeral arrangements and her very best friend so far away? He would have been the best kind of comfort for Madison in her sadness. He was more than a best friend, he was like a brother. Madison didn't have any brothers or sisters, which was one of the reasons her parents decided to get her a dog. The bond between girl and dog was immediate.

Her parents had taken her to the local animal shelter to adopt her new best friend. They looked at every size and shape of dog. Big ones, little ones, fat ones, skinny ones, scraggly ones and smooth ones. But when she laid her eyes on the lone German Shepherd sitting quietly at the back of his kennel, his eyes begging to come out, she knew and *he* knew they belonged together. The dog was already grown; a year and a half old. The man at the animal shelter said that most big dogs come into the shelter after they're about a year old, once the former owners realize the cute things the dog did as a puppy aren't so cute once it's big, powerful and eats like a horse. The man took them into a small visiting room, just to make sure the dog and the family were a good match, but Madison didn't need to visit. After the family decided this was the right dog for them, her father went to do the necessary adoption paperwork while she and her mother waited in the visiting room with the dog. It seemed like her father had been gone forever. She wanted to take her new dog home and she wanted to do it right now!

When they were finally able to leave the shelter and arrived at their car, the dog jumped in, laid down in the seat next to Madison, put his head on her lap and fell fast asleep. Madison ran her hand through the dog's thick, soft fur the entire ride home. He was perfect, just perfect. She couldn't wait to get home and call her grandmother with the exciting news. Her grandmother had always been an animal lover and would be anxious to hear all about their new pet.

But that was two years ago, and now here they were on the way to her grandmother's funeral. As they were leaving the house, Madison's mother didn't know which one looked sadder; her daughter or the dog. Madison noticed that her dog had the same sad eyes he had in his kennel at the shelter that day long ago. She figured he must have known they were going to be separated for longer than a day. With crocodile tears blurring her eyesight, she gave him a long hug and big kiss and walked solemnly to the car. As her parents drove away, her face was pressed against the window as she cried and waved to her beloved dog. Little did she know what lay in store for him while she was gone.

Chapter 2

Missing Bogey

Madison had been feeling blue since they left their driveway. It was a five-hour drive to her Grandma's house and she cried at least half the time. Instead of the typical road trip questions most kids ask, such as, "Are we there yet?" Madison kept asking her parents about her dog Bogey.

"Do you think he's alright?" was her first question. They reassured her that Bogey would be fine and that their neighbor, Mrs. Wells, would be checking on him at least three times a day.

Next Madison asked, "Do you think he's lonely? What's he going to do all day without me there?" At this her parents told her that he surely misses Madison and he's probably getting into all sorts of mischief like raiding the garbage can and rearranging the couch cushions.

Madison's questions went on and on. What if he gets scared? What if Mrs. Wells forgets to check on him? What if there's a storm? A fire? A tornado? An earthquake? The farther they were away, the more dramatic the questions became. When they finally pulled into Grandma's driveway, it was very late and Madison had fallen asleep.

The next morning while her mother was on the phone and her father was beginning to box up some of Grandma's things, Madison once again started with the questions. After spending the morning answering her questions and reassuring her that everything was just fine, her father finally said he would call Mrs. Wells after lunch to check on Bogey. At that, Madison's eyes brightened as if the sun had just risen in them. Her father made them all some lunch while her mother continued to talk to family and others about the funeral arrangements.

After what seemed like her whole life, Madison's mother finally got off the phone. Mr. Sarnicki, Madison's father, took the phone and called Mrs. Wells. The phone rang and rang, but no one seemed to be answering. Then she heard him leave Mrs. Wells a message. Madison would have to wait a little while longer to get the reassurance she needed that her dog was all right and missing her as much as she was missing him.

Chapter 3

A Ray Of Sunshine

It was a cloudy, dreary Saturday, and Kylie was bored. She dreaded cloudy days.

On cloudy days, the grayness seemed to seep inside her house and dampen the color of life as well. Her toys seemed dull and lifeless on days like this. She moped on the couch by the big picture window, twirling her long, mousy-brown hair and trying desperately to figure out how to pass the time. How she wished a ray of sunshine would escape the clouds and brighten her day!

She decided to walk down to her friend Jilly's house to see if she wanted to play. Grabbing her coat, she yelled to her mom that she was going to see Jilly and would be back in an hour.

As she opened the storm door, something quickly jumped up in front of her. Startled, she hopped back into her doorway. What could that have been? After a few tense seconds wondering what she saw Kylie slowly lifted up on the tips of her toes so she could peek through the window part of the door.

There he was. He was big, brownish, with pointy ears. He was sitting on the porch, head cocked to one side, large tongue panting, looking straight into her eyes. It was a dog.

A very large, very muddy German Shepherd dog! He was wagging his long tail, and his eyes looked very happy to see her.

Kylie loved dogs, so she opened the door just a few inches and stuck out her hand so the dog could sniff her. He put his cold, wet nose into the palm of her hand. She decided he seemed friendly, so she opened the door wider and came out to meet him in person. He lay down as soon as she came out. Again, the dog nudged her palm with his nose. She scratched him under his chin, and he stretched his neck closer to her and licked her cheek to show his appreciation for her affection. She noticed the dog didn't have a collar or ID tags on, so it wouldn't be easy to find his owner. She sat down on the moist concrete top step of her front porch, and started rubbing the rest of his damp, muddy coat.

"Boy, you sure are a mess," she told him as she tried to pick the clumps of mud out of his fur.

"What have you been doing, mud-wrestling?" The dog whined a little and laid his paw in her hand, as if he wanted to introduce himself properly.

"Where did you come from?" she asked the friendly dog. "Do you belong to someone around here?" The dog inched even closer to her, licked her hand and rolled over on his back.

Kylie wondered if he was hungry and thirsty.

"Stay here," she told her new friend, "I'll go find you something to eat and drink."

She ran back into the house and flew into the kitchen. She opened the cabinets and grabbed two of her cereal bowls. She filled one half full with water. Since she didn't have a dog of her own, she didn't have any dog food. She opened the refrigerator and took out some bologna. As she was putting the bologna in the other bowl, her mom came into the kitchen.

"Kylie, what are you doing?" her mother asked, wondering what Kylie was doing with a bowl of water and a bowl of bologna. "I thought you were going to Jilly's house."

"Mom, guess what?" Kylie said, almost out of breath with excitement. "There's a big German Shepherd on our front porch! He doesn't have a collar, so can we keep him?" she pleaded with her mother.

Chapter 4

Looking For Home

They had been through this a thousand times before. Kylie begging for a dog. Her mother explaining, once again, that she was too busy to have another responsibility. Besides that, they didn't have the money to properly care for a dog. Kylie's mother worked as a teacher's aide during the day and went to college at night, and it was all she could do to take care of the three of them. Kylie also had a little brother named Tyler who loved animals as much as she did. She and Tyler constantly pestered their mother for a pet.

Reluctantly, her mother said, "You may give him water and bologna, but then leave him alone so he doesn't think this is his new home."

Kylie carefully took the bowl of water and bowl of bologna out to the dog. As soon as she set the bowls down on the ground the dog devoured them.

"Oh, you poor thing!" Kylie said sadly. "You must not have a home, or you wouldn't have eaten so quickly!"

Kylie decided to take her new friend four houses down to meet Jilly, her best friend. Jilly loved animals, too, except Jilly had pets of her own. Happily, the dog followed Kylie down the sidewalk. Halfway to Jilly's house, Kylie decided the dog needed a name.

"I think I'll call you Champ." she told the dog matter-of-factly.

When Jilly answered her door, she was surprised and delighted to meet Champ.

"Where did he come from?" she asked her friend.

"I don't know," Kylie answered, "but my mom said to leave him alone so he would go back to his own home."

"I have an idea." said Jilly. "Why don't we walk around the neighborhood and see if we can help him find his way back home." Jilly grabbed her coat, and the three of them started walking around the neighborhood.

They knocked on several of their neighbor's doors, asking if they knew to whom the dog belonged. Nobody seemed to recognize the large German Shepherd. They walked down Chase Drive from the top of the hill, around the two curves to the bottom of the hill, but still, nobody knew the dog's owners. As they were walking back to their houses, a light rain started to fall. Kylie knew she couldn't take Champ in her house, so she decided to ask Jilly to take him out of the rain.

"Oh, Kylie, I can't; Wags doesn't like other dogs." Jilly informed her friend.

Kylie was stumped. She knew her mother wouldn't allow Champ to come inside, but she just couldn't let him stay out in the rain after all he'd already been through. Kylie knew she'd have to think of something, and quickly.

Chapter 5

Squirrel Trouble

Mrs. Wells was beside herself with worry. Last night she had gone over to her next door neighbor's house to let their dog out one last time before bed. She and Mrs. Sarnicki had become good friends over the past years. When she received the call from her friend needing a favor due to the unexpected death of her mother, Mrs. Wells did not hesitate for a moment. She was at their house often enough that she and Bogey were like family, too.

Oh, how Madison adored that dog! She knew the little girl would be just as upset about leaving her dog as she was about losing her grandmother. Mrs. Wells assured Madison that she would take care of Bogey as if he were her own. Madison made Mrs. Wells give her the scouts honor.

Now, Mrs. Wells didn't know what to do. The child just lost her grandmother, and now the person she entrusted with her most precious possession has failed her miserably.

Bogey was just finishing his business when a squirrel ran by. Next to being with Madison, harassing the neighborhood squirrels was his favorite pastime. Mrs. Wells laughed as she watched Bogey give chase across the yard. She wasn't worried about him running loose because the yard was fenced. When Bogey didn't come back after a few minutes, Mrs. Wells slowly realized that he may no longer be in the backyard.

"Booooo-gey, here boy!" Mrs. Wells called out.

Bogey didn't come. She began walking in the direction Bogey had run. She continued calling his name, calmly at first, but more panicked as she came to the gate.

The gate! She had forgotten to lock the gate! She had brought the garbage cans from the curb earlier and forgot to lock the gate behind her! Panicking, she ran out of the gate, running through the front yard, into the neighbor's yards and down the street, calling Bogey as loud as she could.

After realizing he didn't seem to be close by, she ran back to her house, grabbed her keys and jumped in her car. He couldn't have gone far. It had only been about five minutes, hadn't it? She was so angry with herself for being so careless, especially in a time of such sadness for her friend's family. She would drive around all night if she had to. She just hoped and prayed Bogey would be safe until she found him.

Chapter 6

Hiding Champ

As Kylie and Champ walked back to her house, she tried to think of a plan to convince her mom to let him come in until the rain had stopped. Walking up her driveway, she noticed the car was gone. Her mother must have gone to run some errands.

Suddenly, Kylie had an idea! She would bring Champ inside and hide him in the basement until the rain stopped. Her mom would never know, and as soon as the rain stopped, she'd have Tyler distract her mother so she could sneak Champ out of the house. It was a grand plan that was sure to work!

Kylie took Champ inside, walked him down to the basement, put him under her brother's train table, and moved boxes around the outside of the table so Champ couldn't come out. Her mother only came downstairs on laundry day and she had just done the week's laundry the day before. It was perfect! After refilling the water bowl, she put it down for Champ, gave him a kiss, and told him to lay down and be good until the rain stopped.

But the rain didn't stop. It rained, and it rained, and it rained! The gutters in the street were swollen with rainwater. Kylie was starting to get worried about how to get Champ out of the basement. She knew he probably had to go to the bathroom by now, but she couldn't take him outside.

Her mother had come home from her errands and was so busy she hadn't noticed Kylie was spending a lot of time in the basement. When she finally called Kylie for an afternoon snack, Kylie came up the stairs as quietly as she could, hoping her mother wouldn't notice where she'd been all this time. Just as Kylie was opening the basement door, her mother turned away from the cupboard to put something on the table.

"Oh!" her mother said, not expecting Kylie to come through the basement door. "What were you doing down there?" she asked.

"Just playing," was Kylie's reply, hoping her mother would not notice the guilty look on her face.

As the three of them sat down to snack on some chips and salsa, a large thunderbolt cracked like a whip, making all of them jump.

"Aaarrrooooo!" came a wail from the basement.

"What was that?" Tyler asked excitedly, as their mother asked the same question with a look of confusion on her face.

Kylie, trying to mask the horror she felt when she heard Champ wailing from the basement, tried to distract her mother.

Noticing the look on Kylie's face, her mother said "Kylie, did you take that dog into the basement?"

Sheepishly, Kylie admitted she had, but tried to explain that it was only until the rain had stopped.

"Kylie!" her mother shouted. "I told you to leave that dog alone; his owners are probably worried sick about him!"

"But he doesn't have an owner, Mommy!" she cried to her mother.

"Oh, and how do you know that?" her mother demanded.

Kylie explained that she and Jilly had spent an hour walking through the neighborhood, asking if anyone knew to whom the dog belonged. Then she told her mother no one recognized him and he ate and drank so fast, he must not have a home of his own.

"Well, THIS isn't his home, either!" her mother protested. "As soon as we're through with our snack, we are taking this dog to the animal shelter so his owners can find him."

Chapter 7

The Mysterious Call

Every time the phone rang, Madison would anxiously look at whomever answered it to see if Mrs. Wells was finally calling. Unfortunately, all the calls had to do with her grandmother. Calls came from her aunt, the florist, the funeral director -twice, the water department, and a friend of the family offering her condolences. Everyone seemed to be calling; everyone, except Mrs. Wells. Madison was getting more worried with each phone call. The calls continued throughout the day.

On Saturday evening, one of the calls seemed different in the things her father was talking about.

He said things like "What happened?" and "Who else have you contacted?"

When Madison asked him whether or not he had been talking to Mrs. Wells, he told Madison it was a problem with her grandmother's funeral arrangements. Somehow, Madison didn't think it had to do with her grandmother.

She was right, but her father didn't have the heart to tell her the truth at a time like this. He quietly motioned her mother into another room to explain the situation. Mr. Sarnicki told his wife that Mrs. Wells had called in tears. She explained how Bogey had chased a squirrel towards the gate and how she remembered too late that she had forgotten to latch the gate earlier that evening. She continued by telling him how she drove for hours last night looking for Bogey, and that she hoped he wasn't like the two dogs and cat in "Homeward Bound" that tried to find their family by scent.

Next, she informed him she had spent the day looking for him and posting "Lost" flyers within a five-mile radius of their homes. She reported Bogey lost with both the police department and the newspaper. She had also attempted to call the Animal Shelter, but every time she called the phone was either busy or she got stuck in an endless voicemail system. By the time she actually had the time to drive the forty-five minutes it took to get to the animal shelter, they were already closed for the day and were also closed on Sundays. Finally, she apologized over and over and over again.

Quite frankly, although he loved the dog and was very concerned, there was too much going on with his mother's death to deal with their lost family pet at this particular moment. He and his wife decided they would let Mrs. Wells do what she could and if Bogey hadn't been found by tomorrow, they would break the bad news to Madison. She was already saddened by her grandmother's death and having to leave Bogey behind. If he was lost forever, she would never forgive her parents, Mrs. Wells, and maybe her grandmother. Worse yet, Madison would be completely heartbroken. None of them were in the right state of mind to deal with another major loss in their family.

Chapter 8

The Animal Shelter

After finishing their snack, Kylie, Tyler, their mother and Champ got into the car and drove to the animal shelter. When they arrived, there were lots of people in the lobby. Some of them wanted to bring their pets into the shelter and some wanted to adopt an animal from the shelter.

Kylie's mother walked up to the counter and explained the situation. The person behind the counter, who was called an Animal Care Attendant, listened sympathetically to Kylie's mother explain Champ's story. Once she had finished, the Animal Care Attendant thanked Kylie's mother for bringing Champ in, but said that Saturday is the shelter's busiest day and they didn't have any room for him right now.

"Would you be interested in fostering him for a day or two until we have a cage available for him?" the attendant asked Kylie's mother.

"Fostering him?" she asked, "What exactly does that mean?"

"Well," the attendant explained, "you would take him back home with you and we would call you when a cage opened up here at the shelter."

Kylie heard the attendant and jumped up to the counter. "Can we Mom? Can we please bring him back to our house?"

"Oh, honey," her mother said, "we just can't. We don't have any dog food, and there's no place for him to sleep," she explained to Kylie and the attendant.

"He can sleep with me," Kylie offered. "Tyler and I will make sure we feed him and take him outside to go to the bathroom. I promise I'll take good care of him, Mommy, really I will!" Kylie said convincingly.

"What if his owner comes to look for him?" her mother questioned.

"Well," piped in the attendant, "we will take his picture, write down a description of him and get your information so we can call you if they come in while he's at your house."

The attendant continued, "We can also provide you with some food if you need it, since you're helping us out." Kylie's mom was stumped. She wasn't sure it was a good idea, but the look of hope in her children's eyes was just too much for her.

"How long will he be at our house?" she asked the attendant.

"I'm sure we will have a cage open by Monday or Tuesday." the attendant reassured Kylie's mother.

"Well, he is a very sweet dog, so I guess we can try." she reluctantly told the attendant and her children.

"YIPEE!" Kylie and Tyler shouted with joy.

"Did you hear that, Champ?" Kylie asked the dog. "You get to come back to our house for awhile!"

While Kylie's mother gave the attendant the information, another attendant came and took Champ's picture. Kylie listened carefully as the attendant explained to her mother how the foster program worked. After finishing all of the paperwork, the first attendant handed Kylie's mother some dog food.

"Thanks again for fostering him," the attendant said gratefully. "If it wasn't for good-hearted animal lovers like you helping with our foster program, a lot of animals would be in real trouble."

Chapter 9

More Bad News

On Sunday morning, Madison woke up and immediately ran into the kitchen to see if her parents had heard from Mrs. Wells yet. Her mother and father looked at each other and Madison knew right then that something had happened to Bogey.

"Where's Bogey?" she cried. "What happened to him?"

Her parents both hesitated.

"Mommy, Daddy, please tell me. Is Bogey okay?"

Her mother asked Madison to sit down at the table for breakfast. Madison was getting very frustrated now.

"I'm not sitting down until you tell me what happened to Bogey!" she said boldly.

"Madison, I'm afraid Bogey is lost right now. He chased a squirrel on Friday night and got out of the gate. Mrs. Wells has been looking for him ever since," Madison's mother said quietly. Madison couldn't believe her ears. She just knew something bad would happen if they left Bogey at home. She knew she should have put more pressure on her parents to bring Bogey with them.

Her mother went on, "Mrs. Wells has been driving around in her car, talking to neighbors, putting up lost posters. Honey, she's doing everything she can."

"I want to go home!" wailed Madison. "I want to go home right now and find my dog."

"Honey, we can't," explained her father. "Today we have Grandma's funeral and then we have to tie up a few more loose ends. I'm afraid we're just going to have to trust that Mrs. Wells is doing everything she can until we get home tomorrow."

Madison, very angry with Mrs. Wells for losing her dog, said, "Well *she's* the one who lost him, so she'd *better* find him!"

With that, Madison ran out of the kitchen in tears. Her parents knew they shouldn't have told her today of all days, but Madison was always good at recognizing when they were keeping something from her. Either way, it was a no-win situation.

Madison's mother came into the spare bedroom of her Grandmother's house where Madison was staying.

"Madison, honey," she said with tears in her eyes, as she put her arms around her daughter. Madison pulled away, angry that her parents wouldn't go home right away to find the dog that they all loved.

"I'm sure," her mother continued, "that Bogey will be found. Daddy and I love Bogey and are worried about him, too, but honey, we just can't leave right now. I promise we will leave first thing tomorrow morning for home. In the meantime, we will keep in contact with Mrs. Wells to see if there's any good news, okay?"

Madison hugged her mother and tried to feel better in the safety of her mother's comforting embrace. She really wished that it was she giving the comforting embrace to Bogey.

Chapter 10

Champ's Staying!

Kylie couldn't wait to get home. First, she would get Champ all settled, and then she would call Jilly and tell her the good news. Jilly would be so surprised that Kylie was allowed to keep Champ, if only for a little while.

"The first thing you must do," her mother said, "is give that dog a bath. He is not going to make a muddy mess in our house!"

As soon as their car pulled up in the driveway, Kylie, Tyler and Champ jumped out and ran to the door.

After waiting impatiently for their mother to get the door open, Kylie and Tyler took him down to the basement to give him a bath. Kylie went to the linen closet and found some old towels to dry him with and an old blanket for Champ to sleep on, since her mother already said he couldn't sleep on Kylie's bed. Tyler went to his toy box and found an old tennis ball for Champ to play with. Champ seemed pretty happy to be back as well. Once he did that, Kylie went to call Jilly. As soon as Jilly answered, Kylie yelled into the phone "Guess what, Jilly, Champ's staying!"

"He is?" Jilly exclaimed, "But I thought your Mom wouldn't let you have a dog."

"Well," Kylie explained, "we took him to the animal shelter so his owners could find him, but they didn't have enough room at the shelter, so they asked us if we could foster him."

"Foster him?" Jilly asked, "What does that mean?"

Kylie explained to her friend that the animal shelter had a foster program where people could take care of animals if they got sick, or needed extra attention, or if they didn't have enough space at the shelter.

"Cool!" Jilly said. "I wonder if my mom and dad would let me do something like that?"

In the meantime, Jilly decided that she would help her friend take care of Champ until he had to go to the animal shelter. Kylie asked her mother if Jilly could spend the night since it was Saturday

FOSTERING CHAMP

and they didn't have school the next day. Her mother agreed, and a short time later Jilly arrived with her overnight bag and a brown paper bag stuffed with goodies.

"What's this?" Kylie asked while helping her friend get in the door with her overstuffed bags.

"I brought some stuff for Champ that Wags doesn't like." Wags was Jilly's little Chihuahua mix dog. "There's a squeaky toy, some treats, a rope, a chewy, a collar and a leash."

"Wow, thanks, Jilly!" Kylie exclaimed to her friend.

Jilly said, "Well, I knew you wouldn't have any dog stuff here, so I figured I might as well bring them for Champ."

Kylie picked up the squeaky toy and squeaked it. Champ's ears perked up. He lowered his head and upper body, and woofed. Kylie threw the toy and Champ raced after it. He slid on a rug in the kitchen just like a baseball player sliding into home, and slammed right into the cabinets. Undeterred, he scurried up with the squeaky in his large mouth and ran back to Kylie and Jilly. This made Kylie and Jilly laugh and laugh. They continued to play this game for about thirty minutes.

Then they decided to take Champ for short walk. Kylie loved walking Champ. She felt really important walking such a large dog on a leash. She also felt very protected. Oh how she wished her mother would let her have a dog of her own! She loved how Champ looked, she loved how he felt, she loved that when he was sitting next to her he always wanted some part of his body to be touching hers. Dogs are magical beings.

Kylie, Tyler and Jilly spent the rest of the afternoon and evening doing things with Champ. They played fetch with him in the yard. They played hide-and-seek, Champ being a much better seeker than he was at being the one hiding. No matter where they hid, Champ would always find them in no time at all. They taught Champ tricks like roll-over and shake. He was so smart he learned the tricks after two or three tries.

After a busy day of play, they were all tuckered out and the four of them lay down to watch a movie before bed. When it was time to go to sleep, Jilly helped Kylie make the perfect bed for Champ in the corner of her room right next to her bed. As soon as Kylie laid down the blanket, Champ scratched at it and moved it around before lying down and making himself at home. If Champ couldn't sleep *with* them; at least he could sleep close enough that when Kylie hung her hand over the side of the bed, the first thing she would feel was Champ's soft, comforting fur.

FOSTERING CHAMP

This had been the best day of Kylie's life, and she secretly hoped the animal shelter would forget they had come in, and would never call for Champ.

Chapter 11

A New Morning

A warm, wet muzzle awakened Kylie on Sunday morning. At first, Kylie didn't know what was happening. She had forgotten that she had a large, furry friend in her bedroom. After rubbing the sleep out of her eyes and finally opening them, nothing made her happier than to see Champ's face nuzzling up against hers.

"You must need to go outside, huh?" she asked him cheerfully. Champ gave her a little whine and walked over to the door.

As she and Champ walked into the kitchen, Kylie's mother looked up, surprised.

"Wow," she said to her daughter, "I didn't know you were even capable of getting up this early, much less to do something productive."

Grabbing the leash, Kylie smiled at her mother and replied, "I have to take care of my baby."

She took Champ outside as her mother watched from the window. Her daughter really loved having that dog around.

"He certainly is a good dog," she thought to herself, "and he's great with the kids. Maybe we should think about adopting him if his owners don't reclaim him."

Thinking of his owners suddenly made Kylie's mom feel sad. A dog this wonderful surely has a family out there that loves him dearly. It's going to break her kids' hearts when Champ has to be returned to the shelter. She decided that it wouldn't do any good to think about that now; she might as well cross that bridge when they come to it. Just then both Jilly and Tyler came into the kitchen.

"Where's Champ?" they both asked.

"He's outside with Kylie," she replied, "he had to take care of his business."

"I'm going out to help," Tyler piped in as he opened the back door.

"Me, too," Jilly added, following her friend's little brother outside.

"Good morning!" Kylie called out to Tyler and Jilly as they walked towards her.

"I'm so glad the sun is out this morning," Jilly said.

"It's because Champ's here," Kylie replied. She picked up the tennis ball and threw it across the yard. Champ ran over, picked it up and started trotting back towards Kylie.

"This is fun helping animals, isn't it?" Jilly asked her friend. "I think I'd like to do this more often."

"Well," Kylie said, "I'd like it a lot more if I could help Champ by giving him a new home."

"Kylie," her friend said softly, "what are you going to do when it's time to take Champ back to the animal shelter?"

"I'm hoping my mom falls in love with him, so when the animal shelter calls we can say we've decided to keep him," Kylie told her friend matter-of-factly.

"But Kylie," Jilly replied, "what if the shelter calls because they found his owners? You wouldn't want to keep him from his family, would you?"

"Jilly," Kylie said with hurt in her voice, "I thought you're my friend. We've been having so much fun with Champ, and now you're just making me sad. I thought you're on *my* side!"

"I am, Kylie, but I would hate to see you get really super attached to Champ and then have him taken away," her friend explained.

"Jilly," Kylie said again, still hurt by her friend's good intentions, "I plan on having as much fun as possible with Champ so he won't even want to go home. Tomorrow we have to go to school, so I'm going to make the most of having the whole day with Champ. If you don't want to join us, that's fine, but Champ and Tyler and I are going to enjoy the sunny day together."

"I'm sorry," Jilly said, hugging her friend. "I want to spend the day with you guys, too. Maybe we should ask your Mom if we could take him to County Line Park. It would be cool to take him for a walk on that nature path through the woods, wouldn't it?"

Hearing that, Kylie perked up, smiled at her friend, and ran into the house to look for her mom.

"I really hope we get to keep Champ," Tyler told Jilly. "Kylie and I have been asking our mom for a dog for so long, and she really seems to like him."

FOSTERING CHAMP

"Tyler," Jilly said, looking at him, "Champ's a really great dog. I hate to say it, but like I just told Kylie, I'll bet his owners are going to come looking for him. I wouldn't plan on him being here for very long, and especially not forever."

Tyler frowned at his sister's friend and started walking back to the house. Like Kylie, that was exactly what he didn't want to hear.

Chapter 12

The Worst Day Ever

Madison's mother woke her up early Sunday morning, and Madison was in a bad mood. They had a lot to do before the funeral. Madison had a feeling that her lost dog was not going to be high on the list of things to do.

"Mom, did you call Mrs. Wells yet?" she asked her mother in a groggy, impatient voice.

"No, Madison, I haven't had time," her mother replied.

"Figures!" Madison said in a snotty tone of voice and stomped down the hallway into the bathroom.

"Madison Sarnicki, you get back here right now!" her mother commanded her.

"I understand you are upset about Bogey, but that does not give you the right to speak to me in that tone of voice. We will call Mrs. Wells and check on Bogey in a little while, but Daddy and I have some last minute things to do before we go to the funeral and we expect your cooperation."

Madison didn't want to cooperate. She didn't want to go to the funeral. All she wanted to do was go home and find her dog.

She wasn't really thinking about her parents' sadness and the things they needed to get done. If you asked her, she would say the family dog should be the *only* thing everyone was worried about. "Obviously they don't care very much about Bogey," she thought to herself. "I wish Grandma was here. She'd help me convince them to go find my dog."

That's when it hit Madison. Like she'd just been run over by a truck, Madison broke down in uncontrollable tears. Her mother came rushing out of the bedroom.

"Madison, what happened?" she asked with great concern.

"Mom, what am I going to do?" she wailed.

"I'm never going to see Grandma again, and I probably won't ever see Bogey again!" she cried, trying to catch her breath to get the words out. "This is the absolute worst day ever!"

Her mother cradled Madison into her arms, rocked back and forth and rubbed her daughter's hair.

"Oh, Madison," her mother said, her voice breaking. "Honey, I know this is hard on you. It's hard on all of us. I'm so sorry that there isn't anything else we can do right now."

"But there is, Mom, we can go home and look for him!" Madison exclaimed, a new round of tears falling.

"Madison, listen to me," her mother continued, taking her daughter's face in her hands and tilting it up towards her own face.

"We have to take care of things for Grandma. We'll go to the church, then to the cemetery, and then there'll be a luncheon. When we get back, Daddy and I have to finish things up. We'll all get a good night's sleep and then *I promise*, we will leave first thing in the morning, okay?"

Mrs. Sarnicki knew it wasn't okay, but there really wasn't anything else she could do. Her heart ached for her daughter and for the loss of her mother-in-law, but her hands were tied. Madison was just going to have to try to be strong for one more day. She would do her best to keep her daughter distracted and comforted throughout the day. She prayed that, by some miracle, Nancy Wells would call her with some much-needed good news. Until then, they just had to get through today.

Chapter 13

The Best Day Ever

They were all piled into the car on their way to County Line Park. It was the most beautiful fall day. The sun was shining; it's warm rays taking the crispness out of the morning. The gold, green, orange and red leaves on the trees were like a picture in a magazine. The best part of all, of course, was enjoying all of this with a new dog.

After their mother parked the car, Kylie, Tyler and Jilly jumped out and headed for the two-mile nature trail. The trail wound through the woods around a calm lake at the park. There were a lot of people at the park today, enjoying one of the last days of nice weather before Old Man Winter blew in his long winter chill. There were kids playing catch, a father and son fishing off the pier, and lots of people walking and jogging along the nature path. Kylie held the leash while Tyler walked next to Champ, petting his head. Jilly and Kylie's mom followed close behind, both picking up pretty leaves, dropped acorns and other treasures offered by the forest. Kylie and Tyler started jogging with Champ.

"Don't get too far ahead of me," their mother warned.

"We won't!" They both said, while jogging a little bit faster than they should have.

"Hey, wait for me!" Jilly shouted after them.

Kylie's mom watched the children's joy. Once again, she thought about how happy her children were having this dog around and considering keeping him if possible. Because of Champ's size, Kylie's mom also felt she and her family were protected, should anyone ever give them any trouble.

She was watching her children jump and skip when Tyler suddenly tripped over Champ while trying to pull some leaves off a tree. He fell forward on his hands, skinning them. Tyler was trying to be brave and not release the tears he wanted to let out.

Champ made a little whimper and immediately lay down next to Tyler. While Tyler sat there moaning, Champ gently tried to lick the scrapes on Tyler's hands. As their mother approached, she was awestruck by the dog's immediate sense of caring. She couldn't believe that he would come to her son's rescue so quickly.

"Good boy, Champ," she said, patting and rubbing the fur on his head and neck. She bent down to check her son's hands.

"Mom, did you see that?" Tyler said excitedly, forgetting about his injury for a minute. "Champ tried to make me feel better!"

"I know," said his mother. "He's a pretty awesome dog, isn't he?"

"Yeah!" all three kids exclaimed.

Their mother hesitated for a moment and then said, "Well, maybe Champ should be a part of this family."

Kylie and Tyler froze. They couldn't believe their ears.

"Do you mean it Mom?" Kylie said with guarded excitement.

Their mother realized that she might have spoke too soon.

"Well," she said, "*if* his owners don't come back to claim him, I think maybe we can work out a way to keep him."

"Oh my gosh, oh my gosh!" Tyler kept yelling, jumping up and down.

"Jilly, did you hear that?" Kylie looked at her friend, " My mom said we're going to keep Champ!"

"I said *only* if his owners don't come back, kids," she repeated a little more firmly.

Jilly was happy for her friend, but at the same time, something in her gut told her the happiness wouldn't last.

As for Kylie and Tyler, today was definitely the best Sunday ever!

Chapter 14

A Club Is Born

The next morning was Monday, Kylie's favorite day of the week. Kylie loved fifth grade, and couldn't wait to get to school each week. She loved her classroom; she loved her teacher, Mr. Cole, she loved her friends, and she loved feeling important being in the oldest grade in her school. Fifth graders ruled; everyone knew that.

On this Monday, however, Kylie wasn't happy about going to school. She didn't want to leave Champ. She wondered what he would do all day without her. Her mother said Champ would have to stay in the basement where he couldn't ruin anything. Kylie had brought down his blanket, all the toys Jilly had brought over, and his bowl of water.

She had let Tyler feed Champ that morning so Tyler could feel like Champ was his dog, too. Secretly, though, she really didn't want to share Champ with anyone. The only reason she let Tyler help was in case the animal shelter couldn't take Champ. If that happened, she would need Tyler to help her convince their mother to keep him.

When she got to school, Jilly came running up to her in the hallway.

"How's Champ today?" she asked.

"He's great, but I'm not," Kylie sadly told her friend, "I miss him already, and I'm worried he'll be sad without me home with him."

Jilly gave her friend a big hug and told her not to worry. Just then the twins, Lindsey and Jordan, came up. She had known the twins since kindergarten, and next to Jilly, they were her best friends.

"What's wrong?" Lindsey asked Kylie, seeing the sad expression on her friend's face. Kylie and Jilly told them all about Champ, where he came from, what they had been doing with him all weekend, and how Kylie was now fostering him until he had to go back to the animal shelter.

"Wow!" said Jordan. "That's a cool way to help an animal."

"I love helping animals," Lindsey piped in.

"Me, too," Kylie and Jilly piped up in unison.

Kylie suddenly had an idea. "Hey!" she exclaimed excitedly to her friends, "Let's start a club to help animals!"

"That's a *great* idea!" Jordan said, just as excited as Kylie. Then the first bell rang, warning them they had one minute to be in their classrooms.

"Ok, let's meet in the field at recess and figure out a name for our club and how we're going to help the animals," Jilly said.

Jilly and Lindsey were in one class, and Kylie and Jordan were in the other class, so they could only see each other before school, after school and on the playground at recess.

"Well, we'd better get into class, Ky," Jordan said, pulling Kylie's sleeve towards their classroom.

All morning, Kylie couldn't concentrate on her schoolwork. During English, she sat writing possible names for their new club. During math they were working on money, but instead of doing her assignment about money, it made Kylie think of raising money to help Champ and other animals. Even during Music, which Kylie normally loved, she wondered what Champ was doing in the basement.

When the bell for lunch finally rang, Kylie was relieved that there was only the thirty- minute lunch hour left until recess. She sat down next to Jordan and told her all about the things she was thinking for their club. When the bell rang again to dismiss them for recess, Kylie and Jordan ran to the field on the edge of the playground to meet Jilly and Lindsey. When Jilly and Lindsey got there, Kylie was excited to tell them the name that she and Jordan came up with for their club.

"Animal Survival Group, or A.S.G.," Kylie proudly told them. Jordan smiled and nodded her head.

"ASG," Lindsey repeated. "Well, I guess that'll work."
Jilly piped in, "We can have the meetings at my house when we're not at school." "Great!" said Kylie; knowing Jilly's whole family were big animal lovers.

"We need to decide on jobs," Jordan said, "like on our student council." Both Jilly and Jordan were on the student council.

"We need a President, a Vice President, a Secretary and a Treasurer," Jordan informed them.

"I want to be President," Kylie and Jilly both said at the same time.

"I started the club because of Champ," Kylie protested.

"Yes, but the meetings will be at *my* house, and I gave you all the stuff for him," Jilly answered.

"Well, Jordan and I will be Secretary and Treasurer, so you two will have to decide which one of you will be President and which one will be Vice-President," Lindsey stated matter-of-factly. Just then the recess bell rang.

"Let's talk about it on our way home from school," Jilly told Kylie, knowing they walk home from school together everyday.

When she got back to class, Kylie felt even worse. Not only was she missing Champ now more than ever, but she and her best friend were disagreeing on who would be President of their new club. The rest of the day seemed to drag as slow as maple syrup.

When the dismissal bell finally rang, Kylie met up with her friend in front of the school.

"You can be President," she told Jilly right away. "You're the Student Council President, and you have a dog of your own, so you'd probably make a better President anyway."

"No," Jilly said "You're right, it was your idea, so you should be President."

"Besides," Jilly went on, "the Vice-President is almost like the President, anyway."

"Really?" Kylie asked her friend. "Well, I guess we tell each other everything anyway, so we'll both be making the decisions no matter what our job is." The friends smiled at each other, gave each other a big hug, and walked home.

Chapter 15

A Sign Of Hope

It was noon on Monday and Mrs. Wells was exhausted. She had spent every waking moment for the last 48 hours looking for Bogey. She had continually called the police department and the newspaper to see if anyone had reported a found German Shepherd.

Much to her disappointment, no one had up to this point. She had not had any phone calls from all the flyers she had posted, either. She was, quite frankly, starting to lose hope. She just couldn't forgive herself for making such a foolish mistake and breaking poor little Madison's heart. She didn't know how she was going to face Madison or her parents when they returned home later this afternoon. She couldn't blame them for their anger, really, but she would be sad if she lost a good friendship with Madison's mother because of her carelessness.

She was on her way to the animal shelter next. She drove to the shelter too late on Saturday and it was closed on Sundays, so she was unable to check and see if Bogey had been brought in later in the weekend. The shelter opened at 1:00 today, and she would be the first in line at the door.

On her drive to the shelter, she said a silent prayer that Bogey was there, or at least had been reported. If he wasn't, she was afraid there was nothing left to do. She vowed to continue looking for Bogey as long as necessary, even if it meant making phone calls and visiting the shelter every day.

When she got to the shelter, there were already several people waiting in line at the receiving and lost pets counter in the lobby. There was a woman with a cardboard box full of gorgeous, fluffy gray and white kittens and their beautiful, but stressed-out, mother cat. The owner told Mrs. Wells she was sick of the cat having kittens all the time. Rather than getting her cat spayed, she decided she was just going to get rid of the problem altogether- the cat being the "problem". There was a senior citizen hunched over a cane looking for his beloved Black Labrador-mix dog, which ran away when some mean neighborhood kids opened the gate to let him out on purpose. There was a father and his two-year old boy bringing in a stray cat that had been hit by a car and seemed to have a broken tail. It seemed like she waited for an eternity before it was her turn in line.

When she walked up to the counter, she began to recount the story to a very sympathetic worker. The animal care attendant listened carefully and then asked Mrs. Wells to look through a book that listed found animals while she entered the information into the computer. Mrs. Wells looked quickly but carefully through all the papers in the book. There were many animals listed, but none of them matched the description of Bogey.

Suddenly, the animal care attendant behind the counter perked up.

"Mrs. Wells?" She said. "Can you tell me the area that Bogey was lost in?"

Mrs. Wells told her the closest major intersection to their house.

"Well, Mrs. Wells," she said brightly, "I think we might be in luck. We had a family bring in a German Shepherd on Saturday, but the shelter was full so we asked them to foster the dog until a cage opened up here. The dog matches the description of Bogey and was found about three blocks from the intersection you told me."

"Is it possible for me to see the dog first?" Mrs. Wells questioned. "I would hate to call my friends on their way home from a funeral and tell them we found their dog, only to find out this isn't their dog."

"Yes, you're welcome to do that. We took a picture of him before he went to the foster home," explained the animal care attendant.

"I didn't see his picture in the Lost and Found book," Mrs. Wells informed her.

"If you didn't see the picture in the book, let me check over here in our temporary foster file. We usually make a copy of the picture for the foster file, and put the original picture with the report in the Lost and Found books. If we're really busy, sometimes the original picture and report go into the foster file until someone has a chance to make the copy."

The animal care attendant continued, "If it is the right dog, I will need the owners to come in and reclaim him. It's our policy that I cannot release the animal to anyone except the owners."

The attendant excused herself and a few minutes later came back with the picture.

Mrs. Wells looked at the picture closely. It looked like Bogey for the most part, although the dog in the picture was quite a mess! Still, it looked like him and was found close to where she had lost him. It would be too much of a coincidence for two German Shepherds to be lost on the same day in the same general area, wouldn't it?

Mrs. Wells looked up at the attendant with guarded hope and said, "I think we've got a match!"

"If you're pretty sure that's him, I'll call the finders and see if they can bring him in for you to identify." The animal care attendant went to the phone and called the number of the people who found the German Shepherd. There was no answer, so the animal care attendant left a message.

"Well, Mrs. Wells, I left a message with the people who found the dog. As soon as I hear from them, I will give you a call. I, too, have a strong feeling this is the dog you lost."

Finally, a glimmer of hope! Now she just needed to decide when she should call her friends. Part of her didn't want to call them until she actually saw the dog and knew for sure that it was Bogey. She didn't want to give her friends any false hope, only to disappoint them again.

Chapter 16

Worth The Risk

After much soul searching on whether or not to call her friends, Mrs. Wells finally decided to call them. She felt it was worth the risk of possibly disappointing them. There were just too many factors that made her believe it truly was Bogey. First, he came in the day after he got out of the yard. Second, he was found close to the intersection where he was lost. Third, she saw the picture, and although very dirty, it DID look like Bogey. Finally, and most importantly, her gut told her it was indeed him.

At first, she wanted to make sure her "gut feeling" wasn't really her mind trying to talk her into something that she hoped for but wasn't the truth. But after thinking through all the factors pointing to it being Bogey, she decided to trust her gut feeling. She picked up the phone and called her friends. Mrs. Wells knew the Sarnicki's were already on their way home, but it was a five- hour trip and she had no idea what time they left. She picked up the phone and dialed Mrs. Sarnicki's cell phone number. When Lauren Sarnicki answered the phone, Mrs. Wells took a deep breath before beginning.

"Hi, Lauren, it's Nancy," she began tentatively.

"Oh, Nancy, I was just about to call you," Mrs. Sarnicki replied to her friend. "Have you heard anything about Bogey yet?"

"Actually," Mrs. Wells began, "that's why I'm calling." She continued, "I'm not positive it's him, but I'm pretty sure someone has found him."

"Really!" Mrs. Sarnicki said excitedly. "Where is he now?"

"Well, he's at a family's home," Mrs. Wells replied. "They found him and brought him to the animal shelter on Saturday afternoon, but the shelter was full. The shelter asked the family to take him home and foster him until they had more space."

"Lauren, they found him close to Main Street and Chase Drive on Saturday morning."

She continued, "I did see a picture they took at the shelter. The dog in the picture was pretty muddy, but I still think it was Bogey."

"Well, we're about a half hour away from home," Lauren said. "What do we need to do next?"

"Why don't you call the animal shelter," Nancy said. "They left a message with the finders. Maybe you can arrange to meet them at the shelter."

"That's a great idea!" Mrs. Sarnicki agreed. "I'll call them right now. And Nancy, thanks so much for all you've done."

"Oh, Lauren, I wish there was more I could have done. Actually, I wish I hadn't lost him in the first place!" Mrs. Wells said somewhat sheepishly. Mrs. Sarnicki got the shelter's phone number from her friend. As she dialed the number, she hoped the family's prayers were about to be answered.

Chapter 17

A Prayer Answered

"Mom, did Mrs. Wells find Bogey?" Madison asked excitedly.

"Well, we're not sure yet, Madi," her mother replied with caution in her voice.

"Not sure?" Madison said, the smile of anticipation melting off her face. "What do you mean?"

Mrs. Sarnicki looked at her husband, then turned to her daughter in the backseat of the car.

"Madison, I don't want you to get your hopes up and then be disappointed again," her mother said. "Mrs. Wells thinks Bogey has been found by a family. The dog is staying at their house because there wasn't room for him at the animal shelter. I'm going to call the shelter now to see if we can meet the family there."

"Well, what are you waiting for?" Madison said, a glimmer of hope rising on her face once again. Mrs. Sarnicki dialed the number.

After several rings, a man answered the phone, "County Animal Shelter."

"Hello, my name is Lauren Sarnicki," she began. "We've lost our dog and our neighbor, Nancy Wells, was just in there looking for him."

"Let me transfer you to Lost and Found, ma'am," the man said. Anxiously, Mrs. Sarnicki waited while the phone rang at the Lost and Found desk. After what seemed like fifty rings, a woman finally answered the phone.

"Lost and Found, Lisa speaking."

"Hi Lisa, my name is Lauren Sarnicki," she began again. "My family and I had to go out of town for a funeral. Our neighbor, Nancy Wells, was watching our dog for us while we were gone. Unfortunately, he got away from her. She came in a little while ago to look for him and was told a family came in on Saturday who may have found him."

"What kind of dog did you lose?" Lisa inquired.

"A German Shepherd," Mrs. Sarnicki informed her.

"Oh, yes, I remember," Lisa said. "I helped your neighbor."

Lisa continued, "I called the foster family and left a message. As a matter of fact, the woman just called me back about ten minutes ago."

"She did?" Mrs. Sarnicki asked with relief. "Are they bringing the dog back?"

"Yes, they should be here in about half an hour," Lisa told her. "The woman wanted to wait until her children were home from school. Apparently, they've grown very attached to the dog."

"I see," Mrs. Sarnicki replied. "Well, we're about twenty minutes away from your shelter. Would it be okay if we just came straight there and waited for them?"

"That would be fine," Lisa told her. "I hope it's your dog, but if it isn't then at least you can fill out a Lost Report while you're here."

"Thank you for your help, Lisa," Mrs. Sarnicki replied courteously. "We'll see you soon."

Chapter 18

The Long Wait

"Mom, what's going on?" Madison asked her mother with a look of concern. "Are the people bringing my dog back?"

"Yes, Madison," her mother said reassuringly. "They are bringing the dog to the shelter."

"What if the shelter won't give him back, Mom?" Madison asked, tears beginning to well on her lower eyelids.

"Madison," Mrs. Sarnicki replied, "we aren't even sure it's Bogey."

"But if it is Bogey and they don't want to give him back to us, what will happen?" Madison pressed her mother.

"Madison, Bogey is *our* dog. The animal shelter has to give him back to us," her mother reassured her.

"But what if the shelter people think we're not good owners because we left him with someone who let him get away?" Madison asked, worried thoughts racing through her head.

"What if they think the people who found him loved him more and would take better care of him than we do?"

"What if Bogey is mad at us for leaving him and doesn't want to come with us?"

"What if he doesn't love me anymore?"

"What if…"

"MADISON!" her mother shouted impatiently. "You need to calm down! You're getting way ahead of yourself here. Don't let negative thoughts get the best of you."

Calming her voice quickly, Mrs. Sarnicki explained to her daughter, "Honey, there's no point in getting yourself all worked up over nothing. We won't know anything until we get to the animal shelter and the other family comes with the dog."

Madison quieted down, but she silently cried as she thought of every horrible scenario that would keep her from being reunited with her beloved dog. She would never forgive her parents for not

FOSTERING CHAMP

bringing Bogey with them. She would never forgive Mrs. Wells for being so careless with the most important thing in her world. All she wanted, more than she's ever wanted anything, was to run up to her beloved Bogey, wrap her arms tightly around him and never, ever let go. In a very short time, she would find out the fate of her future.

Chapter 19

The Call Comes

As soon as she walked in the door, Kylie knew something was wrong. Her mother was standing in the kitchen, holding Champ by the leash.

"What's wrong?" Kylie worriedly asked her mother.

"The animal shelter called," her mother told her. "They think they know who Champ belongs to, so we have to take him there right away."

Kylie was absolutely crushed! Gone were her dreams of keeping Champ forever. She hoped and prayed that the people at the shelter were not Champ's owners.

Reluctantly, Kylie, Tyler, their mother and Champ got into the car. Kylie held Champ's leash in her hand while hugging him the entire ride to the shelter. Kylie was so sad, and big crocodile tears fell like a waterfall onto her lap. What if the people at the shelter *were* Champ's owners? How could she possibly hand them the leash? What if they looked mean? Maybe she could just run away with Champ as soon as her mother stopped the car. She thought horrible things about Champ's owners. They had to be bad people, otherwise they wouldn't have lost Champ in the first place.

As the car pulled into the parking lot, Kylie gripped Champ's leash like she was holding on for her life. Her mother came around and opened the door, but before Kylie could protest, Champ jumped out of the car and pulled her out halfway out, too.

Champ looked at the car parked next to theirs and suddenly started barking, whining and pacing back and forth. He walked to the car, sniffed it, then started walking around the car, sniffing the tires, the door handles, the ground by the doors. All the while he was prancing, whining and barking. Kylie actually had a hard time getting him away from the car to go into the shelter. Champ kept looking back at the car, pulling the leash back towards it. As soon as they got to the door and Kylie's mother opened it, Champ's ears perked up, he sniffed the air and started running in. He ran so fast that he pulled the leash right out of Kylie's hand.

"Champ, no!" Kylie cried. "Come back!" she said as she ran after him.

As she was running in after him, a little girl in the lobby broke into tears of joy as Champ ran right into her arms. The little girl's mother and father had huge smiles on their faces as they watched their daughter and their dog being reunited.

Kylie, on the other hand, stopped dead in her tracks. This couldn't be right, she thought to herself. These people didn't look mean, or horrible, or any of the things she imagined Champ's owners to look like, and she certainly didn't expect Champ to belong to a little girl.

Kylie was confused at all the things she was feeling. She was sad that she was losing Champ. She was ashamed that she assumed Champ came from a bad home. At the same time, she was feeling happy, because she saw a little girl find her best friend once again.

"Mr. and Mrs. Sarnicki," the animal care attendant said, "I'd like you to meet Kylie, her brother Tyler, and their mother, Jamie. These are the people who fostered your dog while he was away from your home."

The adults politely shook hands and Kylie and Tyler looked at the little girl. The little girl came over to Kylie and gave her a hug.

"Thank you so much for taking care of Bogey." she said gratefully, "I thought I'd never see him again."

For a moment, Kylie didn't know what to say. She forgot that she named him Champ, so she wasn't quite sure who Bogey was. When her mother touched her on the shoulder, she remembered her manners and said, "You're welcome."

Then Kylie, curiosity getting the best of her, said, "How did you lose your dog?"

"On Friday afternoon, we had to unexpectedly go out of town for a funeral," the little girl's mother explained, "and our neighbor offered to watch Bogey for us." She went on, "She let the dog out in the backyard and while she was taking out our garbage for us, Bogey saw a squirrel and ran out the partially opened gate to chase after it. She feels just horrible about the whole thing. She said she was out for hours calling for Bogey, but with no luck." Mrs. Sarnicki continued, "We've been in touch with her on the phone all weekend. She's been keeping us up-to-date on what was happening."

"Two years ago, we got Bogey from a shelter like this one. When we visited with him before we adopted him, Bogey stuck to Madison like glue. They've been inseparable ever since, with the exception, of course, of this weekend."

Kylie felt better knowing that Champ had a home and a little girl that loved him as much as she did. She knew if Champ were really her dog, she'd be just as devastated if he had gotten lost.

The little girl's mother looked at Kylie and said, "I guess we're lucky good people like you were willing to foster him for the shelter. You should be very proud of yourself, young lady. We're thankful our Bogey was loved and cared for so well while he was away."

Chapter 20

What's Next For The A.S.G.?

Before Mr. and Mrs. Sarnicki and their daughter left, they exchanged phone numbers with Kylie and her family so they could give updates on how Bogey was doing. Kylie was sad to see him go, but she knew he was better off with his own family.

As Champ and his real family were leaving the shelter, she and Tyler each gave him a big hug and kiss. Champ looked at Kylie and lifted his paw as if to shake her hand. Then he cocked his head to one side as he did the day she met him, made a little woof, and gave Kylie the best, sloppiest kiss she had ever had!

After the family left, one of the animal care attendants approached them. "You all did such a good job with that German Shepherd, we were wondering if you'd be interested in becoming volunteers for our shelter and fostering other animals for us," he said.

To Kylie's surprise, her mother said they could probably help out with smaller animals such as cats and maybe small dogs, provided the shelter could help them with food and supplies. She realized that this was a way she and her children could do something good for the community and something they could enjoy together. She also liked that it wouldn't strap their already tight budget, since the shelter would supply the needed food, supplies and veterinary care.

"Great!" said the animal care attendant. "I have a mother cat with a litter of three adorable kittens that could really use some tender loving care until the kittens are old enough to be adopted. If you're interested, we can go ahead and fill out the paperwork for volunteering right now, and send them home with you today."

After filling out the paperwork and speaking with the shelter's Volunteer Coordinator, they brought home a calico cat and her five-week old kittens. One kitten was solid black, one was black and white and the third one was calico like the mother cat. The animal care attendant encouraged them to hold and love the cat and kittens often, so they were used to kids. Kylie was also very excited to find out that the cat and kittens didn't have names, so she was allowed to name them!

As soon as she returned home, she called Jilly and the twins for an emergency meeting of the A.S.G. Their next mission had arrived, and they had a lot of work to do!